The PRINCESS and the BLACK-eyeD Pea

Adapted from The Princess and the Pea

*In a far away land
lived a princess named Breauna,
she was the eldest of her siblings.*

The PRINCESS and the BLACK-eyeD Pea

Adapted from *The Princess and the Pea*

By Deborah Eiland

illustrated by Penny Weber

To my family and friends for their love and support.

In another part of the land lived a lonely
prince named Mosi.

In another part of the palace, Mosi's parents were talking in hushed voices about a plan to cheer their son up.

"We are going to hold a magnificent dinner celebration and invite princesses and princes from throughout the land."

Dinner Celebration

Time   5 p.m.

When   June 16

Where   752 Palace Drive

RSVP

Soon all of the princesses and princes heard of the upcoming dinner celebration for Prince Mosi.

They were talking about what they were going to wear or how they would wear their hair.

The next day Princess Breauna was
so excited she was awake before anyone
and heard footsteps.

She wondered who was awake.

She stepped out of her room.

It was her little brother Prince Azariah.
He saw his big sister and smiled
and gave her a hug.

He looked up and said, "I'm hungry NaNa."

That was the nickname her family
lovingly called her.

She smiled and looked at her brother and said,
"When haven't you not been hungry Za."
Which was his family nickname.

Princess Breauna looked at the clock on the wall and wondered where the time had gone.

Princess Breauna chose her outfit for the celebration because she wanted something semi casual and comfortable while riding her silver Moped Scooter.

It was now time to leave.

Princess Breauna took one final look in the mirror to be sure everything was in place.

Her family waited at the door to wave goodbye while she checked her Moped and placed her lunch in the back covered basket, put on her helmet and rode down the driveway.

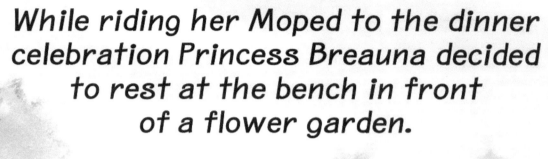

While riding her Moped to the dinner celebration Princess Breauna decided to rest at the bench in front of a flower garden.

There was another person sitting in the
area looking at the colorful flowers.

Princess Breauna smiled and said hello while taking her small lunch out of the back.

She looked at the Princess again but noticed she wasn't looking at her but her lunch.

Princess Breauna smiled and asked, "Would you like some?"

The other princess nodded her head yes.

After a short break, Princess Breauna
continued on the path leading to the palace.

She started thinking about the dinner
celebration and all the things
that would happen.

Princess Breauna arrives hours late with wet hair, clothing muddy and tattered.

She thought about turning around
and going back home but it was now raining
and the sun had gone down.

She tried to put a smile on her face when she rang the doorbell.

The door opened and Princess Breauna saw an elegantly dressed woman she guessed was Prince Mosi's mother.

She looked into the woman's kind eyes and said, "Hello, I am Princess Breauna.

I am so sorry to arrive late but there were events that delayed my arrival."

Prince Mosi's mom brought Princess Breauna into the dimly lit foyer.

Her smile faded and shoulders fell. She feared she was too late for everything.

The elegantly dressed lady rubbed Princess Breauna's shoulder and explained that the dinner celebration had ended a short time ago.

She had insisted that the guests stay the night because it was late and raining outside.

Princess Breauna saw the five soft mattresses stacked on the floor along with a quilt and two fluffy pillows.

As she changed into the clean pajamas left for her, she could feel her body relaxing and began to yawn because of her adventurous afternoon.

Princess Breauna climbed onto the top mattress, slid under the quilt lay her head on the fluffy pillows and closed her eyes.

She felt something poking her back and tried to find a comfortable spot on the mattress

She thought about the things that happened to her before she arrived at the palace.

The next morning
Princess Breauna slowly
walked downstairs.

She had gotten little sleep and her muscles were aching from tossing and turning all night.

The others were already at the table
eating their breakfast they looked up
and saw Princess Breauna
standing in the doorway.

The Queen had a puzzled look on her face.

Princess Breauna quickly explained that she appreciated the bed for the night but tossed and turned all night because there seemed to be a large rock in one of the mattresses.

The Queen jumped up from the table and began swiftly walking towards her.

It looked like she was smiling, almost laughing.

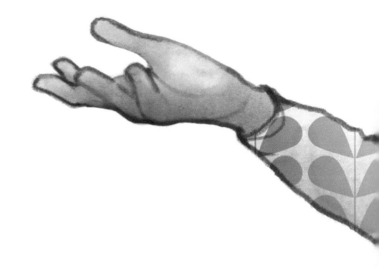

The Queen said, "Come with me."

They went back to the room and the Queen removed the four soft mattresses until only the bottom one was left.

Princess Breauna knew there was going to be a large rock on this one and was shocked when she only saw a small bean.

She shook her head and said,

"This is what kept me up all night?"

The Queen put her arm around Princess Breauna and said,

"This proves you have a kind heart and are aware of the smallest of things."

The Queen knew that her son and Princess Breauna would be friends for a long time but wanted them to discover it for themselves.

They went back downstairs and realized
Prince Mosi had saved

a chair beside him at the table.

CPSIA information can be obtained
at www.ICGtesting.com
Printed in the USA
BVHW012022080223
658147BV00002B/5